"It is Good - CREATION" STICKERBOOK

SABBATH GOD RESTED

AuthorHouse™ UK
1663 Liberty Drive
Bloomington, IN 47403 USA
www.authorhouse.co.uk
UK TFN: 0800 0148641 (Toll Free inside the UK)
UK Local: 02036 956322 (+44 20 3695 6322 from outside the UK)

Because of the dynamic nature of the Internet, any web addresses or links contained in this book may have changed since publication and may no longer be valid. The views expressed in this work are solely those of the author and do not necessarily reflect the views of the publisher, and the publisher hereby disclaims any responsibility for them.

Any people depicted in stock imagery provided by Getty Images are models, and such images are being used for illustrative purposes only. Certain stock imagery © Getty Images.

This book is printed on acid-free paper.

ISBN: 978-1-6655-9564-3 (sc)
ISBN: 978-1-6655-9565-0 (e)

Print information available on the last page.

Published by AuthorHouse 12/15/2021

authorHOUSE®

It is Good - CREATION add stickers

by Kerry Susan Drake

The book is Dedicated to Augustin

Stickers of nature animals and, plants and the stars and planets (heavens) people male and female are a separate purchase. Or cut outs added. An educational early learning book.

It is Good - Creation

The heavens were created
The earth was created
The waters and mountains
The plants and animals
Man slept
Male and Female
It is Good – Creation
Sabbath God Rested

Kerry
Susan Drake

IT

IS

GOOD

Sabbath
God rested

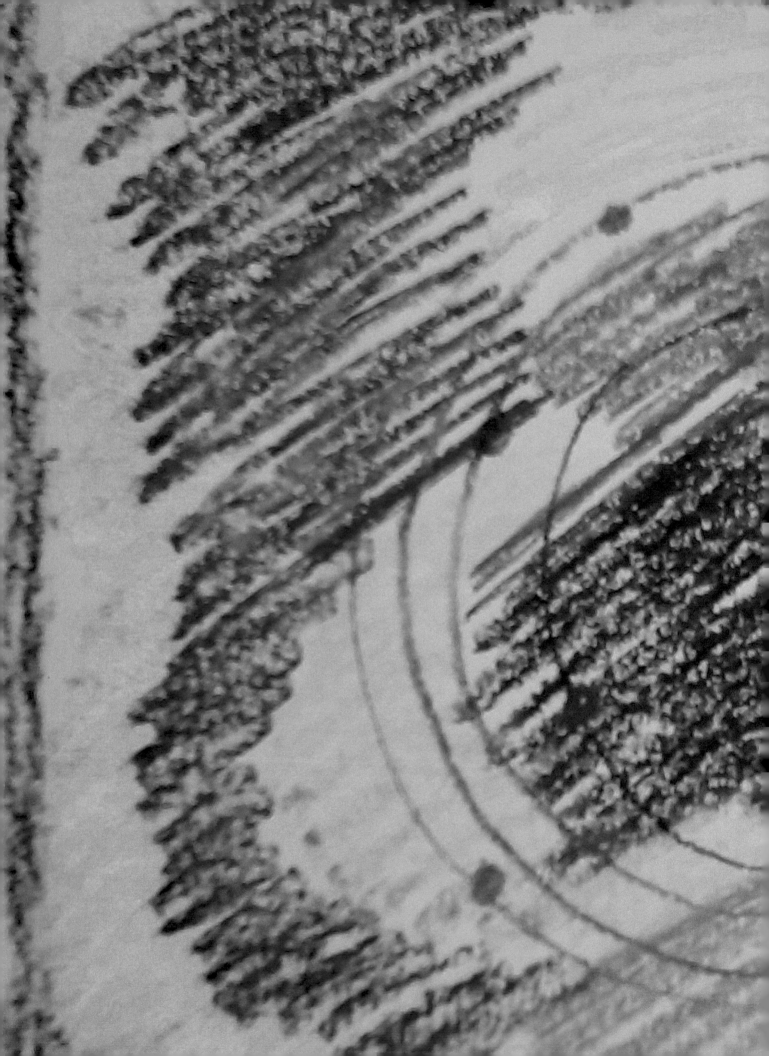

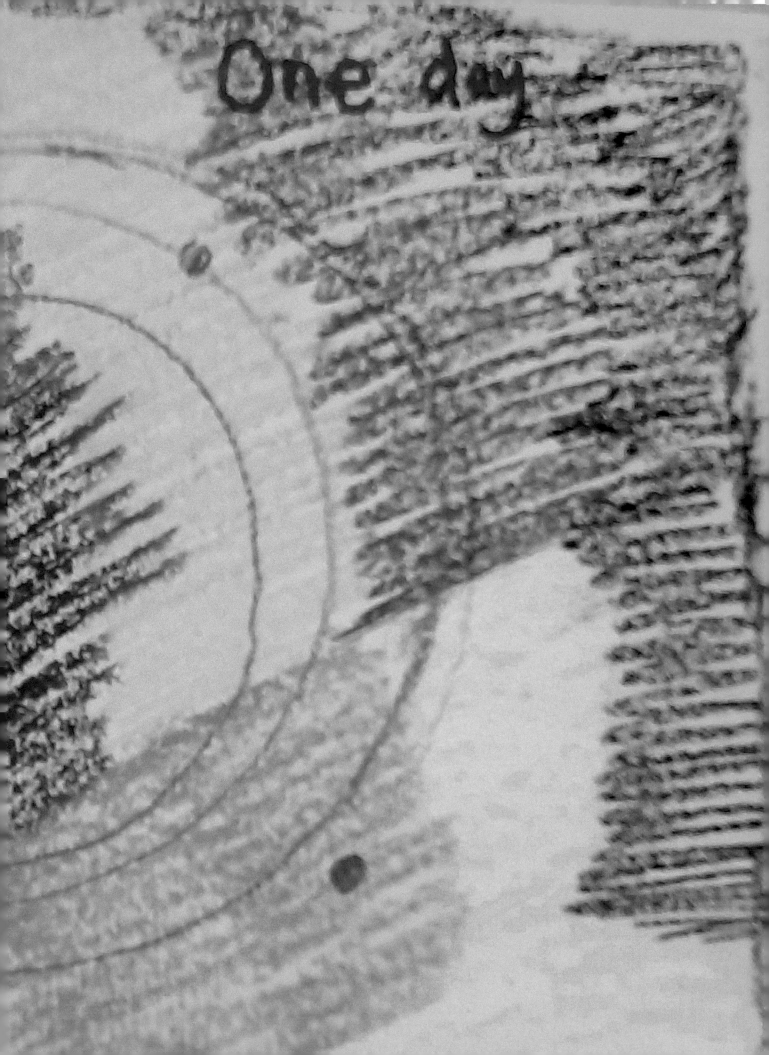

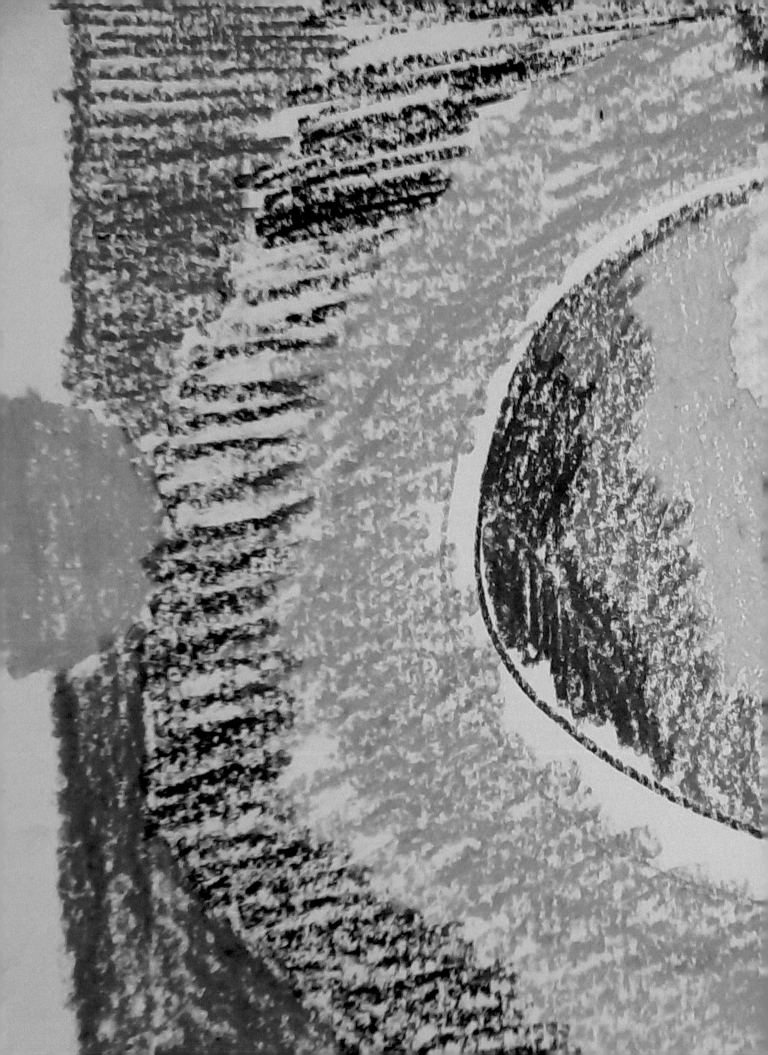

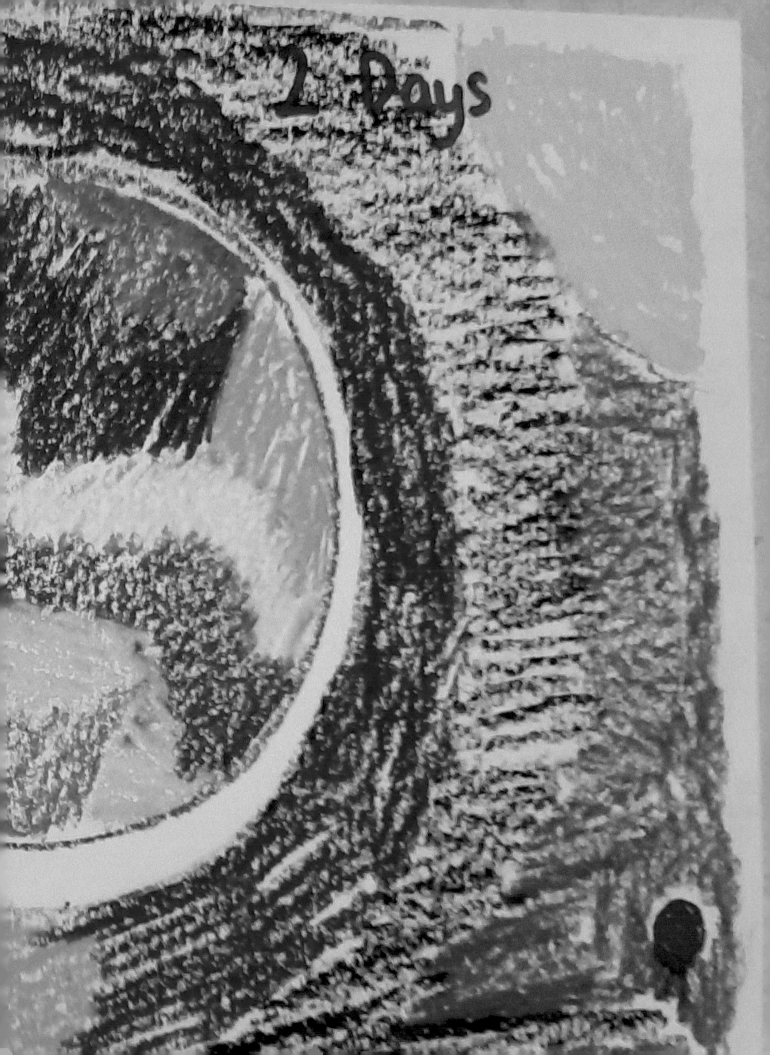

3 days

4th Day

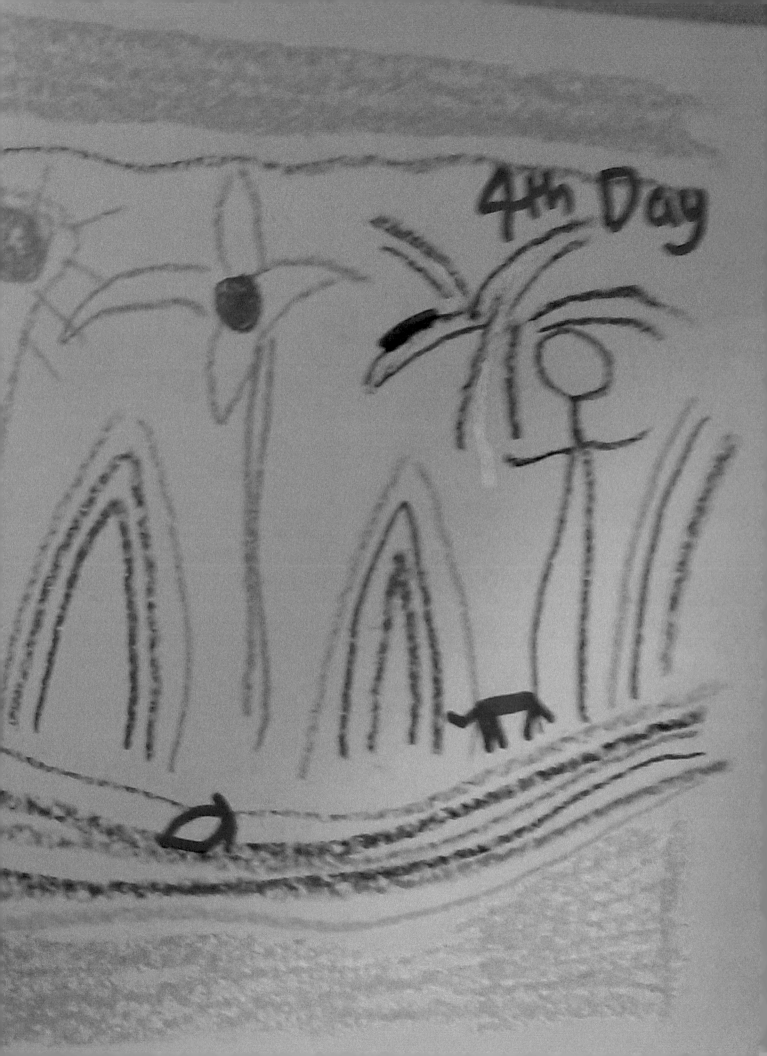

4th Day

Day 6

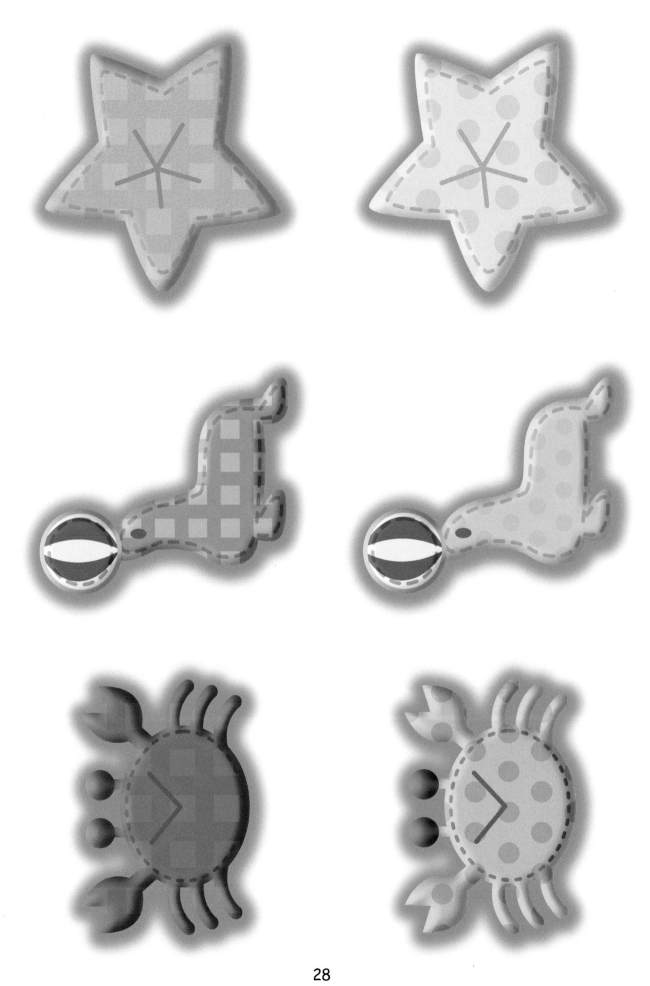

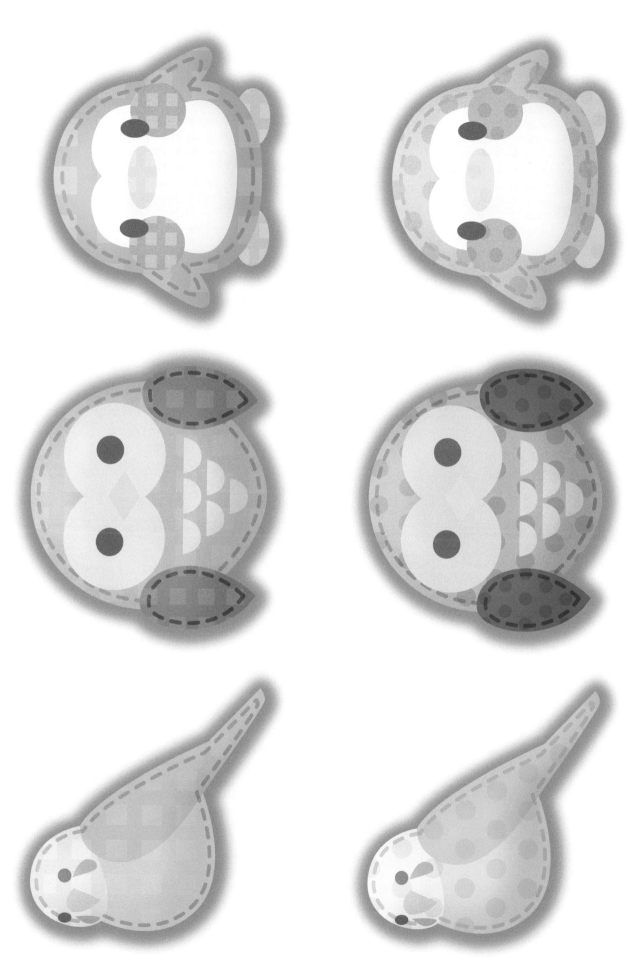

30

ABOUT THE AUTHOR

Kerry Susan Drake as an award winning author celebrates the birth of creation and mankind with a children's book on the heavens, the mountains, waters, animal and plant life, man and male, female.

A creative picture book to add stickers. For children aged 4-8 years old.

Kerry Susan illustrations are colorful and grand giving children pleasure and inspiration to add stickers of the creation.

Kerry Susan Drake MA Writing, Teacher Trinity College London, Graduate Dip Counselling.

Printed in the United States
by Baker & Taylor Publisher Services

"It is Good - CREATION"
stickerbook introduces
children to life, creation and
mankind. It is a colourful
picture book to add stickers
with imagination and
pleasure. A journey through
the creation story.

authorHOUSE®

ISBN 978-1-6655-9564-3

51290

9 781665 595643

THE FOETAL CIRCULATION

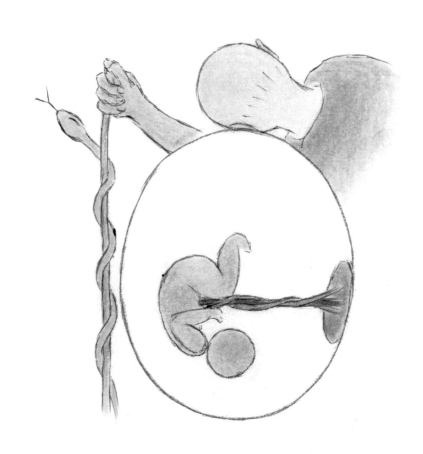

7ᵗʰ edition

Alan Gilchrist